parents and caregivers,

Stone Arch Readers are designed to provide enjoyable reading experiences, as well as opportunities to develop vocabulary, literacy skills, and comprehension. Here are a few ways to support your beginning reader:

- Talk with your child about the ideas addressed in the story.

- Discuss each illustration, mentioning the characters, where they are, and what they are doing.

- Read with expression, pointing to each word. You may want to read the whole story through and then revisit parts of the story to ensure that the meanings of words or phrases are understood.

- Talk about why the character did what he or she did and what your child would do in that situation.

- Help your child connect with characters and events in the story.

Remember, reading with your child should be fun, not forced. Each moment spent reading with your child is a priceless investment in his or her literacy life.

GAIL SAUNDERS-SMITH, PH.D.

STONE ARCH **READERS**

are published by Stone Arch Books
A Capstone Imprint
151 Good Counsel Drive, P.O. Box 669
Mankato, Minnesota 56002
www.capstonepub.com

Children's
Easy Reader

3/11

21.32

Library of Congress Cataloging-in-Publication Data is available on the
Library of Congress website.

Library Binding: 978-1-4342-2063-9
Paperback: 978-1-4342-2800-0

Summary: Buzz and his dog, Raggs, travel to outer space.

Art Director: Bob Lentz
Graphic Designer: Hilary Wacholz
Production Specialist: Michelle Biedscheid

Reading Consultants:

Gail Saunders-Smith, Ph.D.
Melinda Melton Crow, M.Ed.
Laurie K. Holland, Media Specialist

BUZZ BEAKER
AND THE
OUTER SPACE TRIP

Written by
CARI MEISTER
Illustrated by
BILL McGUIRE

STONE ARCH BOOKS
a capstone imprint

Buzz Beaker loves to make cool new stuff. He keeps his ideas in a special notebook.

Dr. Beaker is Buzz's dad. He likes to invent things, too.

Buzz's dog, Raggs, is always excited for new inventions.

Spaceship #5

It was a perfect night. The stars were bright. The moon was full.

The fireflies were blinking.
The crickets were chirping.

Chirp, chirp, chirp.

Buzz Beaker stared up at the
night sky. He sighed.

"If only I could invent a
spaceship that worked!" he
said.

Raggs barked.

"Think of all the things we would see!" said Buzz.

They imagined what it would be like.

"Let's get to work!" said Buzz.

Buzz took out his spaceship notebook. He flipped through the pages.

So far, none of his inventions worked. This one was too small.

This one did not go higher than the mailbox.

Buzz was not sure what went
wrong with his last spaceship.
But he remembered that it hurt.

Buzz threw his notebook in the bushes.

"I give up!" he said to Raggs.

Raggs sniffed the bushes. He picked up the notebook with his mouth.

"I know, Raggs," said Buzz. "A good inventor never gives up."

Buzz opened a new page. He started new plans.

He used his calculator. He used his ruler. He used his brain.

"Time for bed," Dr. Beaker called.

Buzz slowly climbed the steps into the house. He was very tired.

Buzz brushed his teeth.

He zipped up his space
pajamas. He crawled into bed.

Buzz kept thinking about the
spaceship. But soon, Buzz fell
asleep. Raggs did, too.

In the middle of the night, something woke Raggs. Strange sounds were coming from the backyard. *Beep! Zip! Ping!*

Raggs licked Buzz awake.
"What is it?" asked Buzz. "Let's
go see."

Buzz couldn't believe it! Aliens!

Aliens were walking in his
backyard!

There were alien dogs, too!

Buzz grabbed his backpack.
He grabbed his notebook and
three boxes of cookies.

"Now's our chance!" said
Buzz. "Let's go, Raggs."

Buzz told Raggs to be very
quiet. "No barking," he said.

The aliens were busy picking things from the dirt.

It was easy for Buzz and Raggs to sneak onto the spaceship. No one seemed to notice them.

No one noticed them when
the spaceship took off.

Beep, beep, beep.

"This is awesome!" said Buzz.

The ship was just about to pass Saturn when Raggs started barking.

Ruff! Ruff! Ruff!

"SHHHH!" said Buzz.

It was too late!

Raggs ran from his hiding spot to chase a robot cat. The aliens saw them!

Ruff!

Lucky for Buzz, he brought cookies. Aliens love cookies.

The aliens were happy to show Buzz around the spaceship.

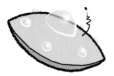

They showed Buzz around their
planet, too. It was very cool.

Buzz woke up in his own bed.

"Was it a dream?" he wondered.

Raggs brought Buzz his notebook.

Buzz started drawing. Then he noticed some writing in his notebook. It said, "Thank you for the cookies!"

THE END

LOOK WHAT BUZZ IS BUILDING!